Mud Tacos!

by Mario Lopez
& Marissa Lopez Wong

illustrated by
Maryn Roos

A Celebra Children's Book

I'd like to thank Marissa, the best sister anyone could ask for!
To my mom and dad, I love you. And my cousin Chico, we miss you. . . . —M.L.

I dedicate this to my hubby—my best friend and soul mate—who inspires me to grow,
and to my three beautiful children, who bring love and laughter to each day.
I also dedicate this to my brother, Mario, who never stops having fun. —M.L.W.

For my big brother, Kevy Lamar —M.R.

CELEBRA CHILDREN'S BOOKS
A member of Penguin Group (USA) Inc.

Penguin Group (USA) Inc., 375 Hudson Street, New York, New York 10014, U.S.A.

Penguin Group (Canada), 90 Eglinton Avenue East, Suite 700, Toronto, Ontario M4P 2Y3, Canada (a division of Pearson Penguin Canada Inc.)

Penguin Books Ltd, 80 Strand, London WC2R 0RL, England

Penguin Ireland, 25 St Stephen's Green, Dublin 2, Ireland (a division of Penguin Books Ltd)

Penguin Group (Australia), 250 Camberwell Road, Camberwell, Victoria 3124, Australia (a division of Pearson Australia Group Pty Ltd)

Penguin Books India Pvt Ltd, 11 Community Centre, Panchsheel Park, New Delhi - 110 017, India

Penguin Group (NZ), 67 Apollo Drive, Rosedale, North Shore 0632, New Zealand (a division of Pearson New Zealand Ltd.)

Penguin Books (South Africa) (Pty) Ltd, 24 Sturdee Avenue, Rosebank, Johannesburg 2196, South Africa

Penguin Books Ltd, Registered Offices: 80 Strand, London WC2R 0RL, England

Text and illustrations copyright © 2009 by Via Mar Productions, Inc.

CELEBRA and logo are trademarks of Penguin Group (USA) inc.

CIP Data is available.

Published in the United States by Celebra Children's Books,
a member of Penguin Group (USA) Inc.
375 Hudson Street, New York, New York 10014
www.penguin.com/youngreaders

Designed by Liz Frances

Manufactured in China   First Edition

ISBN 978-0-451-22751-5

1 3 5 7 9 10 8 6 4 2

One morning at Nana's house, Mario found a big cardboard box. "Hmm," he said. "This has possibilities."

Marissa giggled. Whenever her big brother said that, fun followed!

Mario pulled up a chair next to the box.
"Welcome to my restaurant!" he said.
"Order anything you like."
"I like tacos!" Marissa said.
"Coming right up."

Mario whipped up a batch of tacos with the best ingredients the yard had to offer. The leaves were the shells, the mud was the meat, and there were lots of flower petals instead of cheese.

"*Ewww!*" Marissa laughed. "These tacos are too wormy, squirmy, muddy, leafy!"

Mario's stomach growled. "Let's ask Nana to make tacos for lunch! Meaty, messy, cheesy, spicy, crispy, crunchy tacos. *Mmm-mmm*, tacos!"

There was just one problem. Nana didn't have all the ingredients for tacos.

"No tacos?" Marissa's happy smile flip-flopped upside down.

"Can't we go get what we need, Nana?" Mario asked.

Nana hugged Marissa. "Of course! And we can pick up your cousins, Chico and Rosie, on the way."

Mario made a picture list of the ingredients: taco shells, meat, cheese, lettuce, tomatoes, rice, and beans. "Now you can help find the stuff in the store, too," he said to Marissa.

They walked hand in hand in hand to
Chico and Rosie's house. But only Rosie
was waiting by their front door. "Where's
Chico?" Mario asked.

"BWAHHHHH!"
Chico jumped out from behind a bush
with a scary look on his face.
Marissa jumped back with a scared
look on her face.

"Uh, oh, is little Marissa going to cry?" Chico teased.
Marissa's happy smile flip-flopped upside down.
"Stop teasing her!" Mario said.
"She's the littlest one here," Chico said. "And I'm the
biggest. Being the biggest is the best. Big kids can
do tons of stuff that little kids can't do. And we don't
ever cry!"

At the store, Mario and Marissa, Rosie and Chico looked for the groceries.

"You promised I could push the cart this time!" Rosie said. "You always break your promises!"

Chico rolled his eyes. "Sorry! I'll never break another promise again."

In the checkout line, Nana let the children pick out high-flying balloons. They set off for home. "Let's pretend we're in a parade," said Mario.

"I'm not going to pretend," said Chico. "Now that I'm big, I never pretend."

Back home, Nana sent them outside to play.

"Let's play restaurant again," Marissa said.

"No thanks," Chico said. "I don't want pretend food.
I want real tacos."

Mario nudged Marissa. Marissa whispered to Rosie. "We can make you tacos," Marissa said.

"But if we make them, you have to promise to eat them," Mario said.

"Fine," Chico said. "I promise I'll eat the tacos you make."

"Then close your eyes," Rosie said, "and you'll get a big surprise!"

When everything was ready, Marissa, Mario, and Rosie yelled, "Taco time!" Chico stuck out his tongue. "*Ewww!* I'm not eating that!"

"You have to, you promised!" Rosie said. "And you said you'd never break your promise again!"

"Fine!" Chico lifted the mud taco to his mouth and pretended to eat. "There!"

"Hold on!" said Mario. "You just pretended to eat it.
You never pretend, remember?"

"You eat it first," Chico said to Marissa.
"Oh, no," said Marissa. "I'm too little
to go first. You're the biggest, so you
should go first!"

Chico looked down at the mud taco. He looked up at his cousins. His smile flip-flopped upside down.

"Mud tacos aren't very nice," he said.

"But maybe I should take a bite, because I wasn't very nice today, either."

He picked up the taco. He closed his eyes. He opened his mouth.

"No, no, no!" Marissa knocked the taco out of his hands. She looked into Chico's eyes. She put her hands on his cheeks. "Maybe you weren't very nice today so far," she said. "But today isn't over yet!"

"We can still have tons of fun," Rosie said.
"Just like we always do!" Mario said.
"Just like we always will!" Marissa said.

Chico's smile came back. "I know what I'd like to do," he said. "I'd like to learn how to make something wormy, squirmy, muddy, leafy! Can you show me how to make mud tacos?"

"Welcome to our restaurant!" shouted the cousins.

So Mario, Marissa, Rosie, and Chico whipped up a batch of tacos with the best ingredients the yard had to offer.

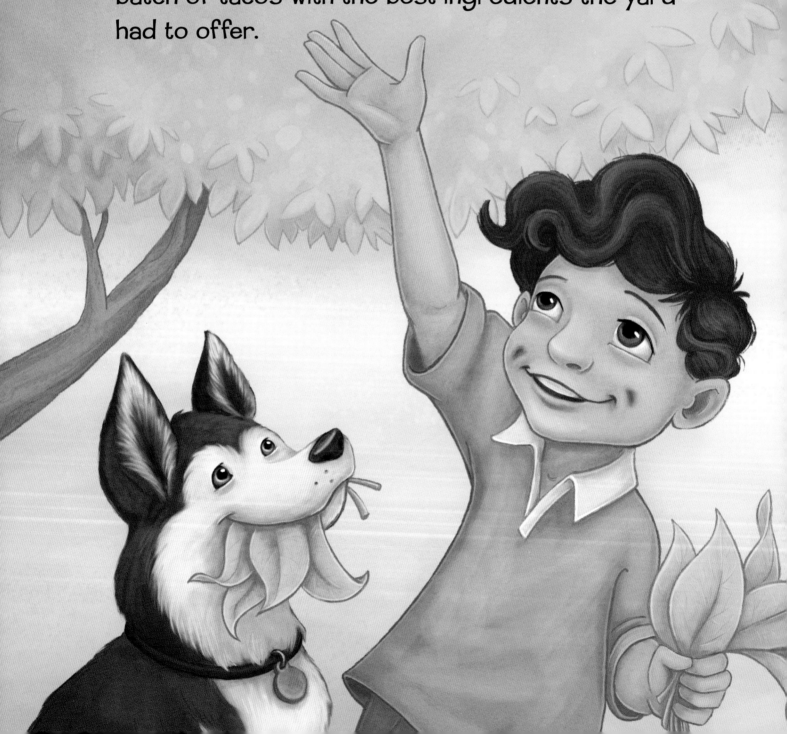

Nana called to them, "Tacos are ready! Time to wash up! Or would you rather have your mud tacos instead?"

Chico picked up the hose.

"No way, Nana!" Mario cried. "Mud tacos are fun to make, but the best thing about them . . .

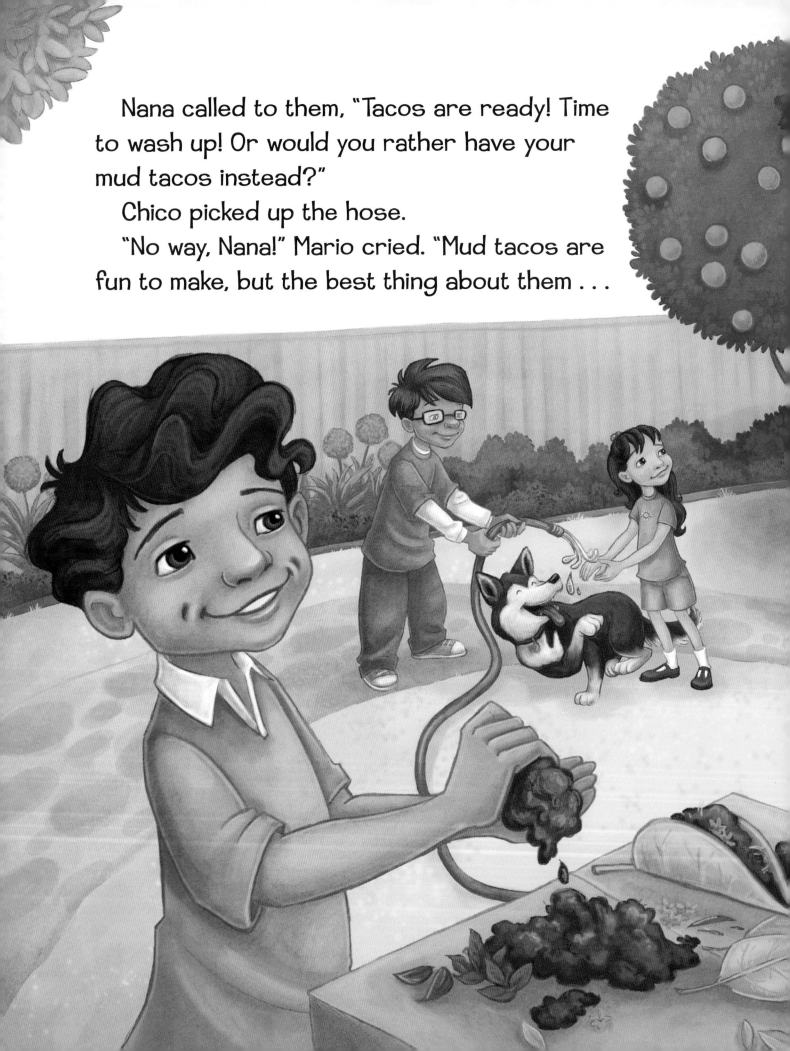

. . . is not eating them!"